"While we try to teach our children all about life,

our children teach us what life is all about."

Angela Schwindt

Good Night Little Lioness Isabella; Katharina Renteria

Copyright © 2014 by Katharina Renteria

Very special thanks to my good friend Deborah Paterson.

ISBN-10: 1512121398
ISBN-13: 978-1512121391

Good Night Little Lioness Isabella

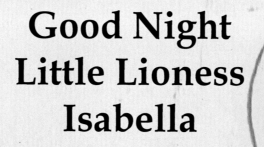

Written and illustrated
by Katharina Renteria

It is late at night,
the moon and stars are shining bright.
Happily, little cats are purring in their dreams.
All over the world it is bedtime so it seems.

High up in the mountains as you can see,
is living a very tired bear family.
They are all sleeping side by side,
cuddling each other through the night.

Even in the dessert in a faraway land
are camels resting in the sand.
All of them have already closed their big dark eyes,
if they hadn't they could see a thousand stars otherwise.

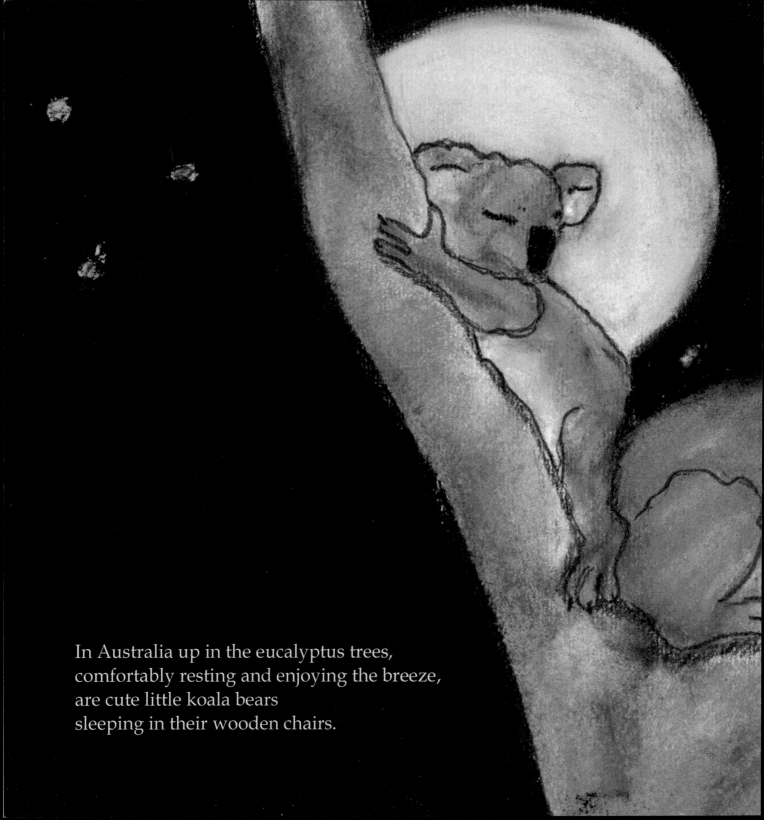

In Australia up in the eucalyptus trees,
comfortably resting and enjoying the breeze,
are cute little koala bears
sleeping in their wooden chairs.

In Antarctica, surrounded by snow so white,
the sea lions are cuddling oh so tight.
All of them tired and sleepy,
now they're dreaming very deeply.

Deep inside the forest, in a hidden place,
wolves are sleeping face to face.
Hush hush, quiet is the night,
they will sleep until the return of light.

There is only one little girl still awake.
Can you hear the noise she makes?
It is a little lioness called Isabella
who is crawling up the tummy
of her very tired mummy.

Her mother says,
shhh, my little girl, don't you see?
It is already bedtime for you and me!
Look at your daddy, can't you hear?
He is snoring and sleeping my sweet dear.

Isabella whispers to her mother,
but mummy, look at the stars and the moon they are so nice!
I do not want to sleep and close my eyes!
All night long I am going to stay awake!
And I will enjoy it with every breath I take.

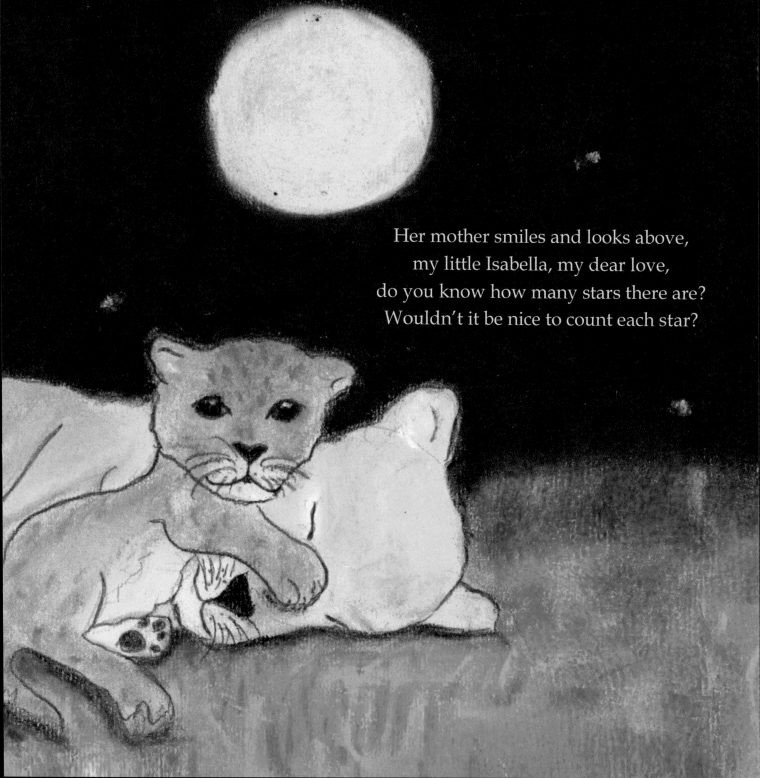

Her mother smiles and looks above,
my little Isabella, my dear love,
do you know how many stars there are?
Wouldn't it be nice to count each star?

So little Isabella starts counting,
one, two, three and four … oh sigh,
five, six, seven, eight … oh my!
Are there no more stars left in the sky?
Look, Isabella can't keep her eyes open
and the last numbers are left unspoken.

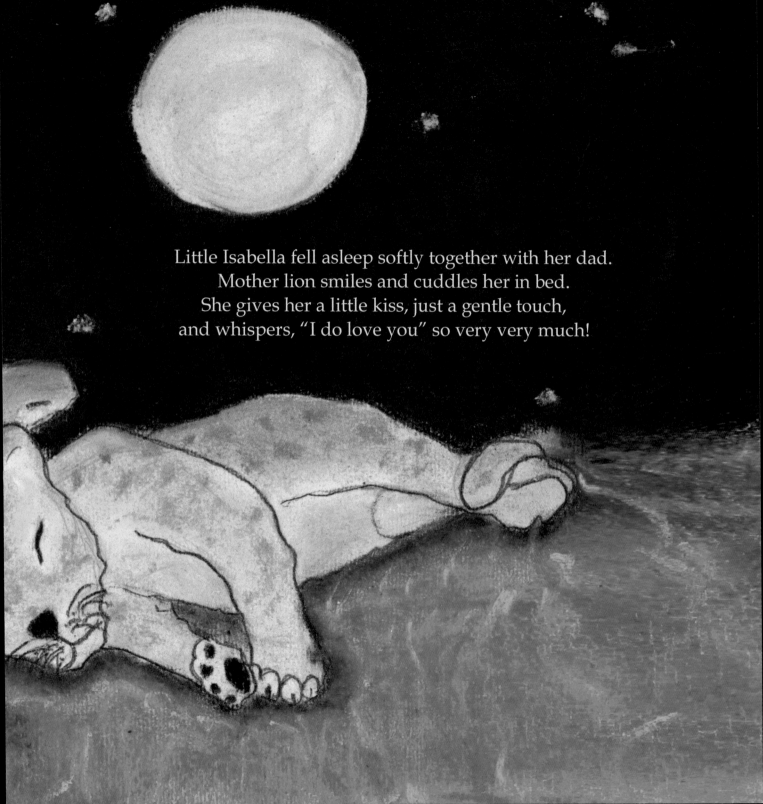

Little Isabella fell asleep softly together with her dad.
Mother lion smiles and cuddles her in bed.
She gives her a little kiss, just a gentle touch,
and whispers, "I do love you" so very very much!

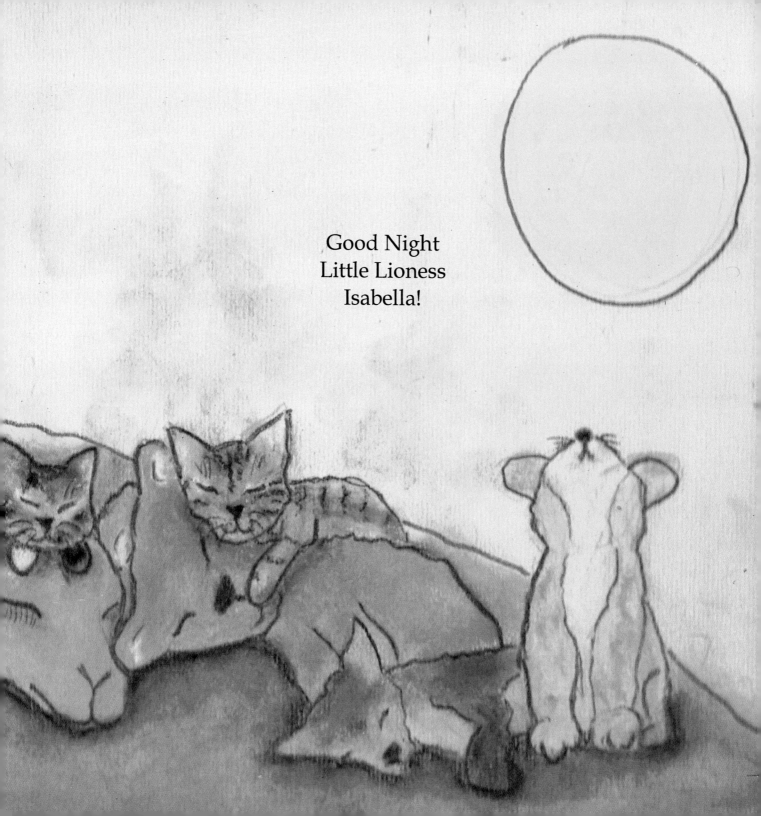

Good Night
Little Lioness
Isabella!

Coming soon by the end of 2015:

Big Brother, Little Sister
Big Brother, Little Brother
Big Sister, Little Sister
Big Sister, Little Brother

A story for children who are expecting
their little brother or sister.